Rhin-O
the
Cybertruck

An Off-Roading Adventure Tale

Written by MOGI Manager of Good Ideas
from Off The GridLock
Illustrated by Jenna De La Paz

Rhin-O the Cybertruck
Copyright © 2023 by Jeanne Carreon
Off The GridLock Publications

Written by MOGI
Manager of Good Ideas from Off The GridLock
OffTheGridLock.com

Edited by Miranda Baird

Illustrations by Jenna De La Paz
www.jennadelapaz.com

First Edition

This book is dedicated to my husband Phil, my unwavering source of support and encouragement. Your innovative and forward-looking perspective have been a huge help on my creative journey. Thank you for being my forever partner in dreaming big.

In a town far away, of dunes, desert, and clay,
Lived twins, Lucas and Oliver, seeking adventures each day.

Their family embarked on an off-roading trip,
In a magical Cybertruck, called Rhin-O, so futuristic and hip!

Rhin-O Rhinoceros, oh what a sight,
Silent and strong with its electrified might.

Underneath the sleek, metal, exterior shell,
Are all sorts of tools that you probably can't tell.

Equipped for camping, overlanding and so much more,
The Rhin-O has gadgets and features galore,

Its tires are huge and all-terrain tough,
Ready to handle any road

smooth

steep

or rough

Off they rolled across trails and steep hills,
Down muddy paths where stream water twills.

Rhin-O climbed over rocks with such power and grace,
With dad at the wheel,no trace of fear on his face.

Autopilot engaged, like a smart helping hand,
The Rhin-O steered true across this great land.

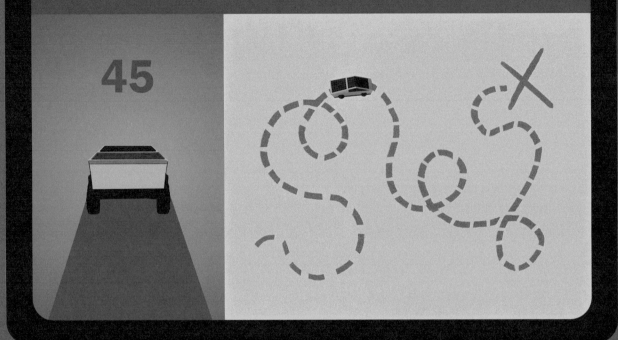

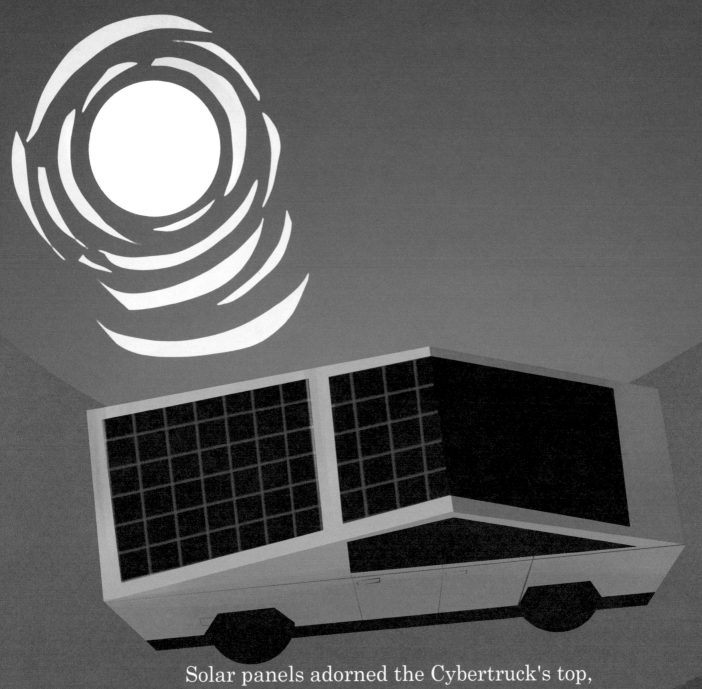

Solar panels adorned the Cybertruck's top,
Harvesting energy, never needing to stop.

As they ventured ahead, a surprise did arise,
A sprawling deep puddle before their very eyes.

Dad couldn't resist and just drove right in,
Splashing muck everywhere into a delightful spin.

"Mud bath for Rhin-O!" Lucas had cheered,
Oliver giggled as muddy splatters appeared.

But worry not friends for mom was a champ,
Rhino-O's built-in shower sprayed out strong, clean, and damp.

Oh the sights they saw as they rambled along,
The Cybertruck hummed like a jubilant song.

They camped by the river under starry clear skies,
Its retractable roof revealed heaven's glorious prize.

They dined on fine meals cooked with artistic flair,
In Rhin-O's mobile kitchen that goes beyond compare.

With cupboards and stoves, it had all that they needed,
To create culinary spreads as their hunger conceded.

But the silliest moment came as such a delight,
When Rhin-O played DJ at their very own campsite.

Its LED lights shimmered in a vibrant display,
With karaoke music to swing and to sway.

Lucas and Oliver sang and moved to the beat,
While their mom and dad showed off their best dancing feat.

The Rhin-O became their party on wheels,
Creating joy and laughter that truly appeals.

Their overlanding adventure silly and bright,
Filled with fun and good times from morning till night.

Lucas and Oliver forever they'll hold,
The memories they made were more precious than gold.

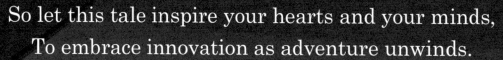

So let this tale inspire your hearts and your minds,
To embrace innovation as adventure unwinds.

Set off on excursions with loved ones in tow,
For unforgettable moments wherever you go.

With Rhin-O the most wondrous Cybertruck to see.
An off-roading journey is waiting for you and for me!

follow along on our real life journey!

 Website: OffTheGridLock.com

 Instagram: @offthegridlock_otgl

 YouTube Channel: Off The GridLock

 Other books by MOGI - Check out *Jack and the Unicorn* on Amazon.

Made in the USA
Thornton, CO
11/14/24 01:12:47

c1a89087-e00f-40f0-9233-05cb7d119f24R01